For Nelly Chambers JW

To Cake-Grandad
(the cheekiest monkey we know) JC

First published 2013 by Walker Books Ltd
87 Vauxhall Walk, London SE11 5HJ

2 4 6 8 10 9 7 5 3 1

Text © 2013 Jeanne Willis
Illustrations © 2013 Jane Chapman

This book has been typeset in HVD Bodedo

Printed in China

British Library Cataloguing in Publication Data:
a catalogue record for this book is available from the British Library

ISBN 978-1-4063-4394-6

WALKER BOOKS
AND SUBSIDIARIES
LONDON · BOSTON · SYDNEY · AUCKLAND

MONKEY FOUND A BABY

Jeanne Willis

Illustrated by
Jane Chapman

A monkey found a baby,
an itsy bitsy baby
A monkey found a baby
beneath the banyan tree.

What did she **feed** the baby,
the slurpy burpy baby?
She fed him squashed bananas
beneath the banyan tree.

What did she **show** the baby,
the wriggly giggly baby?
She pointed to a lion
beneath the banyan tree.

What did she **tell** the baby,
the shouty pouty baby?
She said, "Don't tease the lion
beneath the banyan tree."

ZZZZz

BUT
The baby blew a raspberry,
a rooty tooty raspberry
He crept towards the lion
beneath the banyan tree.

ROOTY
TOOT

WHEEE

He tugged the lion's tail,
the rufty tufty tail
He tugged the lion's tail
beneath the banyan tree.

ROAR

The lion gave a big roar,
"What did you do THAT for?"
The lion gave a big

ROAR

beneath the banyan tree.
AND ...

The lion chased the baby,
the waddly toddly baby
The lion chased the baby
beneath the banyan tree.

SO...

The monkey chased the lion,
the growly prowly lion
The monkey chased the lion
beneath the banyan tree.

UNTIL...

TEE HEE

The lion caught the baby,
the bumbly tumbly baby
The lion caught the baby
beneath the banyan tree.

BUT ...

The baby bit the lion,
the yowly scowly lion
The baby bit the lion
beneath the banyan tree.

THEN...

The baby chased the lion,
the hairy scary lion
The baby chased the lion
beneath the banyan tree.

BUT
The monkey grabbed the baby,
the nippy skippy baby
The monkey grabbed the baby
beneath the banyan tree.

She gave him back to mother,
my dizzy busy mother
She gave him back to mother,
beneath the banyan tree.

BECAUSE...

He is my little brother,
my crazy baby brother
And he's a cheeky monkey
as everyone can see!